LOST CAT

Written and illustrated by C. Roger Mader

HOUGHTON MIFFLIN BOOKS FOR CHILDREN
HOUGHTON MIFFLIN HARCOURT
BOSTON NEW YORK

For Martine and Pete

Houghton Mifflin Books for Children is an imprint of Houghton Mifflin Harcourt
Publishing Company.

www.hmhco.com

The text of this book is set in Cantoria MT.
The illustrations are pastels on paper.

Library of Congress Cataloging-in-Publication Data
Mader, C. Roger.
Lost cat / written and illustrated by C. Roger Mader.
p. cm.
Summary: Slipper the cat is mistakenly left behind in the commotion
when the lady she has always lived with moves in with her daughter's family,
so Slipper sets out to find someone new to adopt.
ISBN 978-0-547-97458-3
1. Cats—Fiction. 2. Lost and found possessions—Fiction.
3. Pet adoption—Fiction.] I. Title.
PZ7.M2569Los 2013
[E]—dc23   2012041891

Manufactured in China
SCP 10 9 8 7 6 5 4
4500573026

Ever since Slipper was a tiny kitten,
she'd lived with a little old lady in a
little old house in a little old town.

Slipper was well cared for: tasty food, a brushing every day, and a little rug to sleep on, right beside the lady's bed, next to the fluffy slippers she loved so much.

Life was good.

Slipper chased the moving van for miles and miles. Finally she got tired, slowed down, and lost the trail.

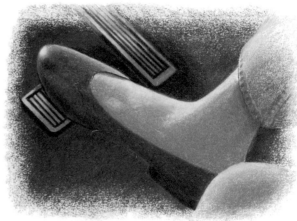

When Mrs. Fluffy Slippers and her daughter realized that Slipper was not in the car, they raced back to the empty house. But the cat was gone.

Lost!

Slipper spent a cold night all alone. She had tried her best to find Mrs. Fluffy Slippers, but now she would look for someone new to adopt.

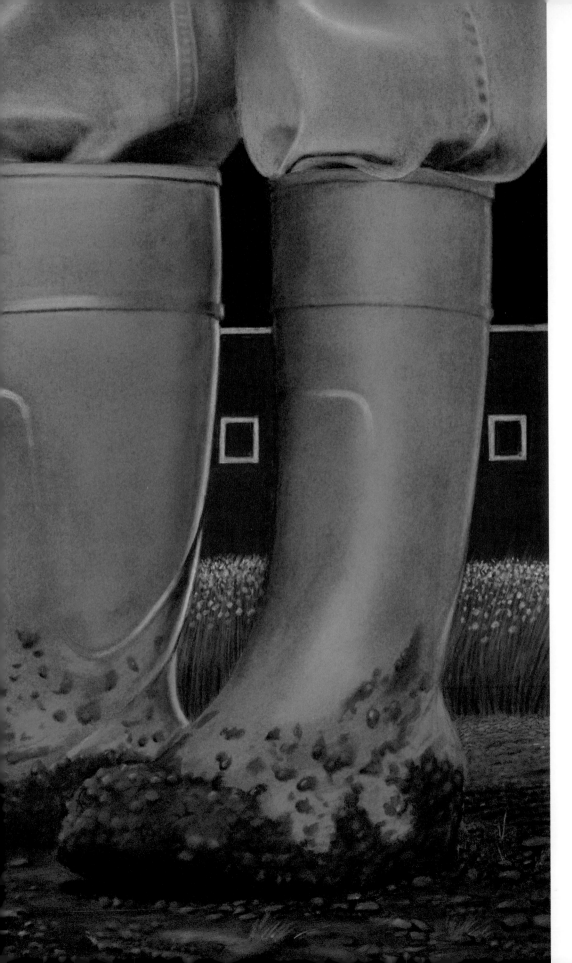

Ms. Muddy Boots was near the road when Slipper passed by.

"Hi, kitty," she said, offering Slipper a fish. Slipper had not quite finished eating when a dog charged out of the yard. She quickly jumped to safety.

She could have adopted the woman, but that dog?

Never.

Mrs. Iron Shoes came clop, clop, clopping along the road. The rider asked Slipper if she would like a lift. But Slipper took one look at the horse's hooves, thought about her own soft little paws, and skedaddled.

Mr. Cowboy Boots was downing a lemonade when he invited Slipper to ride in his truck. But with the smell and all the noise, Slipper meowed, "No thanks," and continued her search.

High Tops jumped out
from behind a bush and
yelled, "I'm taking you
home!" Slipper felt a flash
of fear, and in a heartbeat,
she fled.

Mr. Big Boots arrived with a roar. He scooped Slipper up, scratched her ears, and put her in a saddlebag. After a fast and scary ride, they screeched to a stop at a red light. They were in a town, so she hopped out.

Crouching under a mailbox, Slipper watched the people passing by. When she caught glimpse of a pair of shiny shoes, she knew she had to follow them.

When Miss Shiny Shoes arrived home, Slipper looked up at her and meowed sweetly, "May I adopt you?" The girl opened the door and they walked in together.

This home had a family, and Slipper felt so safe and comfy, she decided to adopt them all.

Miss Shiny Shoes led her down the hallway.

At the bedroom door she said . . .

"Grandma, look who followed me home!"

That night Slipper slept on the same old
rug by the same old bed, snuggled up with
the same old slippers.

Life was good.